PUP IS UP!

Jack Wagger &
Delette Marengo

Archway Publishing books may be ordered through booksellers or by contacting:

Archway Publishing
1663 Liberty Drive
Bloomington, IN 47403
www.archwaypublishing.com
1 (888) 242-5904

ISBN: 978-1-4808-8848-7 (sc)
ISBN: 978-1-4808-8849-4 (hc)
ISBN: 978-1-4808-8847-0 (e)

Print information available on the last page.

Archway Publishing rev. date: 04/02/2020

ARCHWAY
PUBLISHING

PUP
IS
UP!

By Jack Wagger

&

Delette Marengo

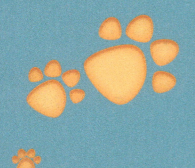

Ring! Ring!
Wake-up Pup!

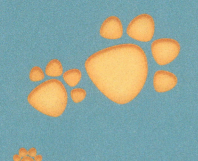

Sleepy puppy …

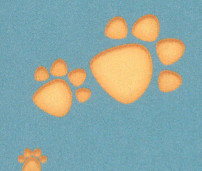

… Pup is up!

One paw!
Two paws!
Three paws!
Four!

Puppy paws are
on the floor!

Puppies don't wear
shirts and pants …

... but puppies do a "wake-up" dance!

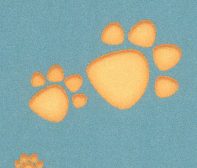

Wash the sleepy …
off my face.

Eat my breakfast …
first say grace.

Mom made Milk Bones …
Clean my plate!
Little puppy … don't be late!

CPSIA information can be obtained
at www.ICGtesting.com
Printed in the USA
BVHW020355110420
577391BV00016B/1157